Locked in Pleasure

SplinterRealm
Nesi L Stone

LostStone Publishing

2nd Edition

PRINT ISBN   978-1-0699517-5-5

EBOOK ISBN   978-1-0697483-3-1

Cover LostStone Publishing

Editing EJL Editing

Formatting LostStone Publishing via Atticus

For me

Cause we all should do things for ourselves

ALSO BY NESI L STONE

TRIGGER WARNINGS

Forced Pregnancy

Sexually explicit

Explicit language

Forced Proximity

Dubious Consent

Dystopian setting

Playlist

Shameless -Camilla Cabello
Unholy -Sam Smith & Kim Petras
Satisfaction - Benny Benassi
Black Widow -Iggy Azalea
Boss Bitch -Doja Cat
Such a Whore - JVLA

Eve

Eve's fingers skated across her computer, putting together the final paperwork to transition her role in her company to a remote one as it was her time to go to the Pod. Her birth-year Pod rotation had been pushed back until later; they were all only one year off from their whole year getting pardoned. *She had been so close.* The extra time had allowed her to build *Printed in Ink* to where it is now. Her exclusive tattoo parlor had its finger on the pulse of the under-city, serving a luxury experience to the powerful players running the city from behind the scenes. Like cockroaches the illegal side of the world had survived just fine, even thrived now.

She closed her laptop, sliding it into her leather work bag. The cafeteria was busy as everyone gossiped about what was to happen, who they might be matched with, or how long they would be in the Pod. Quite a few faces were missing since they had all been in school together three years ago. *Had it really been three years already?* Those who had applied to get a couple pardon, or had already produced a child to the state, were not present. Each person had gone through days of testing to complete a full genetic panel. At least a third of her group would have been flagged as infertile, another reason for the missing faces, and another third would have been prescribed medication to make up for their lower fertility. Then, a month after the testing, everyone had received a letter with the time and date everyone was to appear here for their pairing. Each person in the group was paired with another that provided the most genetically advantageous match. Theirs was the third generation to have not lived through the events of the doomsday that had lead the world to this monstrosity. Still, rampant fertility issues plagued the population, which had not recovered. This was the cure; it had been projected that it would take another three generations to fix the issues. Through careful genetic breeding, humans were becoming GMO.

With 83 percent of the population gone, infertility from the radiation fallout had caused a population crisis. Eve was convinced that whoever came up with the Pod had a breeding kink and was using it as their own personal fantasy.

She tugged at the long sleeves of her shirt, ensuring that they had not ridden up her arms. Being the shy, plain mousy girl who was a little too heavy-set to be popular had aided her in surviving the viper pit of high school. Being surrounded by all the same people again had sent her back to her old ways. Now, though she hid my body for an entirely different reason, gone was the self-conscious girl who hated herself. Replaced was a headstrong woman with a body of art she was proud of, but that pride had to be placed in the back of her mind and pulled out of a dark, dusty corner, where the shy, curvy girl was unfolded. She hated herself for folding back into who she used to be so easily.

The patchwork of tattoos that graced her skin —across her arms, over her shoulders, twisted down her spine, and looped around her legs. Lost in thought over her past, Eve was pulled back to the reality of the moment as a loud bout of laughter filled the room. Looking over at the group in the middle, Xander and his cohorts were fucking around in the center, clearly whatever thought had come to their small little brains had been funny, surely at someone else's expense. Xander looked over at Eve and smirked at her. He had been a plague to her constantly doing things to push her buttons. He found joy in making her uncomfortable at least in high school and it seemed he had not changed.

What a tool. Eve picked up her book, *The Fever of Fortunes by Chris Boff,* flipping to her bookmark. She secretly looked over at Xander as he turned back to his fan club. She told herself she had grown into a successful businesswoman in the three years since she graduated high school but right now she felt right back at square one.

"Who's next for fuck, marry, kill!" Xander boasted. *My gods, that's what they are doing? Of course.* The announcement system crackled to life, letting everyone know to pay attention to their bands that they would light up green when they were selected to proceed to the Pod. Eve glanced down at the thin metal band that looped her wrist. She could not imagine a time when everyone did not sport one. She had worn one her whole life. ID, banking, and medical info were all processed through them. Streamlining every aspect of life.

Despite her distaste for Xander, her heartbeat hammered in her chest as she watched him over the pages of her book. His tall, muscled form as he moved, the way people watched him in awe. The tattoos he flashed with pride along his tan arms. The detailed linework and dark colors were truly magnificent. She was only admiring them as an artist not as a woman. *Obviously.*

He was trouble. It was etched across every inch of his skin, and yet Eve was drawn to him despite herself. She had watched him for years as he grew up from an angry bully to a mysterious bad boy who promised trouble and pleasure in the gentle wink of his eye. They had shared many classes, Eve secretly watching the most popular boy in her grade grow up.

Her bracelet flashed green, and she quickly stashed her book in her bag, glancing back at Xander one last time, who had his back to her. She needed to let her long-time crush on him go. She walked off with her bags over her shoulder, not looking back once she started to walk away. She carted her suitcase with her, everything she would have for however long she was in the Pod.

It could be weeks or months. There was a small line of people waiting at the steel doors leading to the Pod, each with a flashing green band.

Eve waited until it was her turn. She flashed her band at the scanner, and it lit up green, and her band stopped flashing. The person handed her a package of papers, her name typed out on the front, followed by her SIN number. Taking the package, she followed the single hallway as she flicked the first page open. The first page had a floor and room number on it. Floor 124 and Room 67B.

Eve stopped at a wall of elevators, which had a couple of people waiting for the next one. Three people stepped into the elevator and scanned their bands; everyone else was left waiting for the next. Such was life; doors locked until your band un-locked it if you had access. The Pod was a series of halls and locked doors that she had to scan through to ensure everyone made it to the cor-rect room. There was a non-fraternization policy which she found ironic considering the reason for the Pods existence.

Eve stepped into the small metal box, tugging her bags behind her. The walls were flat gray and uniform, broken up by the plain white doors with numbers. Then every several doors, a large window let in bright light, the gloss on the pane blocking the view.

After walking almost halfway around the curved building, Eve came to a door with large black letters stamped on it. *67B*. Flashing her band at the door handle, it clicked, and she slowly pushed the door open. She had not been the first in their group to be shown to her room; there was no guarantee her match would be in the room already, or if they would walk in right behind her. They did not send up each pair together, seemingly randomly sending everyone to their rooms. It could be hours until she met who she was paired with. She tried not to panic at the sight of her door. This room had seen many couples through the generations, just like Eve. The Pod had been built from the ground up for its purpose. The room was empty; the air still. The room was more of an apartment than Eve had thought it would be; like the rest of the building, it was plain and emotionless. Gray and metal, broken up by splashes of white. The place was soulless something her artist heart hurt at.

Eve took in the room before her, first the couch with the TV perched on the wall in front of it; she was surprised they provided entertainment for them. Her attention swept round to the island in front of the kitchen. She was excited about the pantry and relieved to see a washer and dryer almost tucked out of her view around the corner behind the kitchen. Across from her were three plain doors, presumably leading to the two bedrooms. She abandoned her bags in the middle of the room to investigate the rooms, she gently pushed open the first door. She was nosey and she knew it.

A bedroom stared back at her. She felt like it stared back at her blankly. Matching the monochrome look of the rest of the Pod. A bed sat on a rug next to it a dresser, hiding most of the hard-wood floor. Eve ignored the painful bubble of her stomach and walked over to the wall of windows, looking out over the city. She looked down at her home feeling small compared to the vast sea of buildings. Eve walked out of the first room and scoped out the other bedroom. It was a complete mirror of the previous one she had seen. *Great job architect.* Sinking into the bed, she sat there thinking for a moment trying to process the mess of emotions rolling through her. The last door, the one in the middle, was a bathroom.

The white metal tub, with a shower head much to her satisfaction, sat against the far back wall. A matching sink and toilet was tucked against the left wall, they reminded her of something you would find in a design magazine. A round mirror stared back at her, placed on the door of a small cabinet above the sink. A room straight out of an IKEA show room.

It was completely silent in the apartment, even thought the building was filling with other people. Shaking the unnerved feeling from her body, Eve fetched her bags. She started to unpack. Her mind not on the task at hand. *Who would she be paired with?* Sorting her clothes into the dresser. She unfolded the gray fabric cubes she had packed with her, and laughed a little at how they matched the rest of the place. One for her undergarments and one for her socks. She tossed all the toiletries onto her bed, planning to transfer to the bathroom later. Her slightly chaotic but organised to her method of settling into her space in full swing.

Next came all Eve's work items, piled up next to the toiletries on her bed. Computer, calendar, notebook, pencil case, a whole stack of sketchbooks, and her computer stand that was covered in stickers that allowed her to work from her bed, her preferred office. Her mobile office.

She gently placed, next to the pillows, her beloved blue stuffed Dino, the stuffed and weighted child's toy was cuddled up in her favorite blanket, a black and rose design covered in the words *'fuck you'.* She knew she was too old at 21 to be so attached to such items but she didn't care. Eve gently patted the head of her Dino before turning her attention to stuffing her bags into each other, then shoving the lot under her bed. Scooping up all her toiletries in her arms, juggling everything in her arms in one trip, she wobbled over to the bathroom. Half distracted, she kept her ears open, waiting to hear when her match would be joining her. She filled up half the shelves in the bathroom with her items, over packed as always. She was trying to keep her hands busy while her mind raced. Still, Eve was alone, left unknowing of who she would be living with for the foreseeable future, let alone conceive a child with. Who she would be getting naked with and doing the most intimate act with?

Eve flipped through the rest of the information pamphlet. One outlined a detailed map with the routes to the gym, pool, and library that were spread out over the floor. The next one was a list of instructions on how to use the in-built ordering system. As Eve read through the instructions, she wandered over to the panel right by the door. Flipping through the touch screen. This panel would run her life; anything she needed would be processed through here and then sent up to her room if deemed necessary. It was also her way out; to be released from the Pod, you had to submit a positive pregnancy test, which would be verified by a doctor. You submitted it through this panel. All emergency services could be called through this panel. This panel was the lock and key to her life.

One page explained what Eve already knew about the pregnancy and ovulation tests, being especially coded to interact with the panel, and that outside tests were redundant. Finally, Eve got the Wifi password, which she had really been looking for. Before turning from the panel, Eve keyed in a request for groceries. Submitting all her basics and favorite foods. Her match could place his own food order, he would have to scan his band to finalize the order.

The infrastructure of the Pod seeming futuristic compared to real life, showing what can be done with human innovation when effort and more importantly funding was put to a cause. The Pod and its human breeding program being the most important project to the federal government since the radiation fall out impacted the population.

Sitting on her bed, she logged on to the Wifi and pulled up her work email. Eve got lost in the piles of emails that were already waiting for her attention. *Girl Boss Babe and all.* Not even a full day since she had last checked it. Jolted from her work by the sound of the door opening, she glanced at the time, over two hours later. Eve jumped out of her bed, settling her racing heart before she slowly stepped out of her room. Her match was here.

"I already placed an order for food, it's still pending, feel free to add anything you want to it." Eve looked over at the man she would be trapped with; he wasn't facing her, looking over the space they would share. Eve didn't need to see his face to know who he was. The snake tattoo wrapping his arm was enough. *Xander.*

He turned to look at Eve as her stomach dropped. Xander looked her over. Eve was left feeling like cattle up for auction under his gaze. Not that she was far off considering she was here forced into having a child with up until now a random stranger.

"The . . . er . . . paperwork." Xander offered her the papers in his hand. Eve handed over her matching paperwork, clearing both of them of any STIs and all health conditions that were pertinent to their stay in the Pod. Eve stated she was on a mild fertility drug that wasn't uncommon, and neither of them had any red flags in the paperwork. Eve took her time looking over the paper, mildly surprised that he had been cleared. Xander barely glanced at hers. Eve fidgeted with her sleeve, not wanting to break the increasingly awkward silence between them.

"I'm in that room. You have the other one. I'll let you unpack." Eve scurried back to the safety of her room, closing the door, leaning against it, letting out a breath she hadn't realized she had been holding.

Eve wrestled her phone from her pocket, pulling up the endless chat with Cece. Her fingers raced over the screen as she tried to contain all her feelings in words.

Eve

> ***GUESSSSSSSSSS WHO IS MY PAIR!!! FUCKING XANDER!!! WHAT THE FUCK ARE THE ODDS!! HELPP! WHAT DO I DO?! HE IS SUCH AN ASSHOLE!!***

The all-caps did not convey the level of panic pumping through her blood. Cece left her unanswered, but would certainly reciprocate her feelings later. Cece had been one of the first few to be guided up to their rooms. Eve slid down the door, curling up at the base, resting her head against her phone. The door wobbled with the knock.

"Food order is here." Moments later, the sound of his feet moving away twisted under the door.

Gathering herself, Eve stood up and opened the door. Seven black boxes, with the floor and room number printed on them, sat on the floor right by the door.

"Do you want help?" Xander stood with his hands in his pockets, leeching relaxation into the air.

"Sure." Eve opened up one box, pulling out each item. Xander placed each item on the shelf Eve indicated. In under twenty minutes, all seven boxes were packed away, their bare shelves now full.

"Are you hungry?" Xander asked, waving a box of tomato and herb pasta bake around in the air.

"I could eat." Eve nodded.

Eve dug into the piping hot pasta bake, trying not to keep looking up at Xander sitting across from her at the kitchen island.

"Are we gonna talk about it?" Xander asked out of the blue. Eve jumped at his question, confused as to what he meant.

"We can." Eve offered before filling her mouth with the delicious creamy pasta.

"I see several options for us," Xander started.

"We could take the ovulation tests and just fuck when you are ovulating." The way Xander said the word fuck, how it seemed to roll around his mouth and kiss his lips filled with promise, had Eve clenching her legs together.

"I would feel like an incubator or a broodmare." Eve didn't look up at Xander, moving her food around her plate.

"We could go the complete opposite and try being a couple." Eve looked up at Xander, his eyes looking past her and right into her soul, unwavering.

"I'm not sure we need to go that far," she squeaked, looking away from his burning gaze. She regretted the second it left her mouth. She shot down her chance of being with him. She had dreamed of the chance every day in school.

"You are right." He busied himself with his food.

"We live like roommates, but fuck like bunnies until we conceive." She suggested not looking at Xander to hide her face, the slight edge of disappointment and hurt in her tone.

"That works for me." He stood up, clearing away his plate. Without another word or glance her way, Xander retreated to his room. She hated herself for snubbing her shot at the man she had lusted over for years.

Eve put away her dishes, fighting with her emotions, the storm that boiled within her. She tried to settle into bed, but could not sleep. She pulled her book close to her and began reading the words sliding before her eyes losing herself in a world of magic and the story of a woman angry at the world. Slowly, sleep wrapped its reluctant fingers around her.

Eve had left the curtains on the wall of windows open all night. She blinked awake in the soft light of sunrise. It was still very early. She stayed in bed and listened to the gentle sounds of him in the kitchen; she couldn't quite figure out what it was that he was doing. A light knock sounded at her door.

"Yes?" She didn't bother getting out of bed, her legs feeling as heavy as her heart.

"Breakfast is ready," he said through the door.

"Thank you." The promise of food pulled her out of bed. Getting slightly confused over where, in fact, she had unpacked everything, and settled on yoga pants and a cute crochet sweater. Her first layer was a long-sleeved thin bodysuit. She tugged her favorite yoga pants over the flesh-colored body suit that hugged her curves. Throwing the sweater over her head, she peeked to make sure all you could see through the holes in the sweater was the sleeve of the suit. She was determined to keep her tattoos hidden.

Slipping out of her room, she was greeted by a sea of breakfast foods in front of her. Had he made all of this from scratch?

"I meal prep in large quantities. We can box the leftovers up and eat them tomorrow," Xander said, waving at the plates of food. Fruit salad, waffles, pancakes, bacon, eggs, yogurt, sausages, hash browns, and toast. All of it waited, tempting Eve. She smiled at Xander before filling her plate with one of everything.

"Plans for the day?" Xander asked, eating a pancake with his hands.

"Work." Eve tucked her fork into her potatoes.

"Same," Xander said, picking up another pancake. *What did he even do for work?* Eve smiled at him before slinking back to her room. Shutting the door behind her, she picked at her plate of food even after it had long been cold. Sitting in bed, she worked her way through an ever-growing list of issues to solve. This one is a manufacturing issue; getting her hands on the ingredients to make her favored ink for the parlor. Hours seemed to slip by like water; her mind swimming with a confusing mix of emotions she could not name. Eve slipped out of her room to grab more food, her stomach bubbling. Hours later, the sun was low in the sky, a riot of colors in the gray-scape of the Pod. Once again, she was pulled under the ocean of work, coming up for air to shower long after night had fallen. Her brain feeling numb in her skull. Gods she wished for have a tattoo gun in her hand right about now.

Eve fell asleep her muscles finally relaxing, cuddled up with her work. She woke refreshed, hours later, her back stiff and her brain fuzzy. She stumbled out from under her pile of work to find coffee. Her need for caffeine guiding her. Blindly fumbling from her room to the kitchen. Eve looked up to see Xander's back, shirtless, flexed over the coffee maker. She stood there watching the muscles in his back flex as he moved about making coffee. Enjoying the sight of him.

"Morning," Eve mumbled, walking over to grab a mug from the cupboard. Pulling a small gray mug from the shelf.

"Morning," Xander's voice thick with sleep. Eve dumped several spoonful's of sugar into her cup, followed by a healthy splash of milk, filling the remaining space with the fresh coffee. Blowing on her coffee, Eve sipped it lightly, looking over her hot coffee at Xander. He was leaning against the counter, nursing his coffee; however, it was black. Eve admired the contoured muscles of Xander's chest and abs over the top of her coffee.

"How's work?" Xander's voice was still gravelly, but he sounded much more alert than moments before.

"Good," Eve muttered, a dark look in her eye.

"Hungry?" Xander asked, placing his mug, half empty, on the counter.

"Starving." Eve smiled at him, her gaze staying on his face as she too set down her now-empty coffee mug.

"I'm making pancakes." Xander twisted once more with his back to her.

"Yum. I'd love some." Eve secretly watched Xander as he prepared the pancakes. Eve made her way through three more cups of coffee before the plate of pancakes appeared before her.

Eve dug into her syrup and butter-soaked pancakes with gusto. She fought to keep her focus on her food. Xander had pulled out a notebook and was busy scribbling away in it as he ate. She watched as his pen danced across the page, his looping writing sitting somewhere between print and cursive. She wanted the chance to tattoo a quote in his handwriting. She busied herself, shoving a huge bite of syrup-soaked pancakes in her mouth as he put his notebook away. He looked over at her, with her chipmunk cheeks full of pancakes, and started laughing.

"You have syrup all over your face." Eve tried to dab at her face.

"No, not there." He stood up, pointing at her face. Once again, she dabbed at her face, and he continued to laugh at her.

"Right here." His thumb brushed along her jaw and over her chin. His thumb ran up her chin and over her bottom lip. She turned bright red, embarrassment flooding her veins under his touch. He had a wicked look in his eye as a small smirk tugged at his lips lust dripping from his eyes. She battled with her mind to pull her chin out of his grasp, not quite winning. He leaned over, pressing his rosy pink lips to Eve's dry and cracked ones. She sat there stunned, still unmoving in his grip. She relaxed against his lips, their passion heating, melting under his touch. He pulled back, a full smirk in place across his face.

"Are we gonna . . . you know . . . ?" Eve mumbled, trying not to stutter and make a fool of herself. Which she failed at. She felt like a baby deer on ice trying to seem threatening. She was back to being the teenager with a crush on a boy.

"We can," Xander said as he straightened to his full height. Preening under her Xander held Eve's gaze as he pulled at the strings on his black jogging pants. Eve gasped as his pants dropped to the floor, leaving him in the full nude. What her younger self would have done to be in the same room as him naked even a couple years ago and now she was living it.

"It is what we are here for," Xander said, the bemused lilt to his voice giving away his ego. Eve smiled at him as her mind was spinning over how to handle this. Before Eve's brain had found a solution to keeping her tattoos covered, Xander swept his hand over her hip. He pulled her up and out of her chair and up to his chest. He was a good six inches taller than her.

"Ready?" Xander purred in her ear. Eve nodded breathlessly.

Xander tugged at her, spinning her until her back was to him. Xander's hand snaked up Eve's back, bending her over the kitchen island. His large hands palmed her hips, lifting her so her weight rested on the counter. Xander wiggled her sweatpants over her round hips and plump ass. Xander didn't pull them down very far, just enough for him to take in Eve's ass. Enough for him to be able to stick his cock in her.

Eve jumped slightly as Xander's fingers traced the line of her panties, digging into her flesh. She gasped as his finger sliding down between Eve's thighs, sliding under the fabric of her panties, tugging the thin fabric from her cunt. The cold air licked at Eve's wet skin, the pounding heat building between her thighs.

Xander ran his hands over Eve's lower back, and tingling danced up Eve's spine. Gods she felt like she was going crazy in the best way. With one hand pulling the fabric of her panties aside, and his other on his cock, Xander dragged the head of his cock along Eve's glistening cunt. She couldn't even feel the edge of the table digging into her anymore. Eve relaxed into enjoying the moment, realizing Xander had no interest in undressing her anymore.

"Ready?" Xander asked as he gently pressed the head of his cock into the warm entrance to her pussy.

"Yes," Eve breathed her voice quiet. Xander's thumb gently dug into Eve's hip gently Xander pressed his weight into Eve. His cock sliding effortlessly deep into Eve. Eve gasped at the feeling of his cock sliding deep within her, the muscles in her body fighting to accept his size. Her fingers gripped the side of the counter. Xander's hands splayed out over Eve's hips, filling his hands with her ample ass.

"Fuck, you feel so good," Xander whispered before he slowly pulled back. Wisps of pleasure licked at Eve as she felt Xander moving inside her. Her veins boiled with ecstasy.

"Better than I imagined," he mumbled to himself. Eve flexed her fingers right before Xander once again thrust into her, the air pulled from her lungs in a ragged gasp. As Xander sped up with his thrusts, Eve's moans got lost in her lungs as her brain got muddy, as pleasure wrapped its warm arms around her. The muscles in her core tightened as she let go of control and let herself feel. Xander's hands on her hips dug in with a delicious pain, his grip stopping her body from slamming against the counter. Through the fog of pleasure clouding her brain, Eve heard the sound of Xander fighting against his own waves of pleasure flooding his brain. *Fuck.*

"I can't, I'm gonna . . . " Xander ground out as his control was fraying at the edges. The sound of the lust and pleasure Xander was feeling sent Eve over the edge. Eve's orgasm slamming through her body, her legs shaking from the intensity. Xander moaned in her ear as he followed her over the edge. Eve slumped against the counter, her legs still shaky. Xander let go of her hips, resting his hands on either side of her, and resting his chin against her back.

"You ok?" Xander asked against her skin. Eve shifted her feet, testing her weight on them.

"Yeah," Eve's voice even sounded weak to her ears.

"Good." Xander sounded almost breathless. Xander shifted his weight off Eve, and she straightened. Eve didn't turn to face him until her face was no longer blushing. Xander was quiet behind her, not moving but no longer touching her.

"Interesting." Xander's fingers gently brushed the skin just above the left leg of her pants. Eve's heart stuttered; she knew that the skin he had just touched was too low. Some of her ink was showing. Eve quickly tugged her pants up, turning to face him.

"What?" she asked, willing her voice to sound light and confused.

"You have a tattoo," Xander stated, not swayed by her feigned confusion.

"Yeah." Eve's confidence wavered.

"How did I not know?" Xander frowned at her.

"I never showed you." Eve tried to shut the conversation down.

"Can I see it?" Xander stepped forward.

"No." Eve took a step back to match him.

"So we can fuck, and conceive a child, but I can't see your tats?" Xander had hidden his hurt under layers of anger.

"It's not like us fucking means anything. We were just a match." Eve snapped back.

"Right," Xander said, walking off to his room. Eve was left standing there feeling empty. Eve shuffled to her room, ignoring the roaring pain in her heart. Eve sank onto her bed, rolling herself up in the blankets and closing her eyes, willing the tears to stay put.

Eve sank into a deep, dreamless sleep, her eyes fluttering open many hours later. Her room was pitch black. Eve pulled out her phone, checking the time. It was ten minutes past midnight, and she had slept away the whole day. Forcing her stiff muscles to sit up and pull herself from her bed, she made her way to the bathroom. Gently pushing her door open, she quietly padded out of the room. The light was on in the bathroom, the door ajar by several inches. The sound of the shower running wrapped around Eve's ears, her brain taking several moments to understand what she was hearing. Eve sneaked forward to peek in the door to see if the bathroom was occupied.

The bathroom was filled with sage-scented steam, dancing and spinning in the air. Eve glanced around the small bathroom, her eyes turning to the glass doors of the shower. The glass was fogged up, but the outline of Xander was clear through the blur. Eve battled with herself over wanting to watch and prying into his private moment. Eve lost the battle and gave in to sneaking a peek at Xander. It took Eve several moments before she caught on to what Xander was doing in the shower. His hand rested against the glass, his side profile clear to her. He was touching himself. Eve was entranced by him; she watched as his hands slid over his cock, the muscles in his back tense as he worked himself up to climax. *He was jerking off.* Eve's heart pounded in her chest, her blood heated and pooled in her hips. The space between her thighs was growing slick with need.

Did he have feelings for someone else? Was earlier not enough for him?

Eve froze at the sound she heard coming from the bathroom. Xander was moaning softly. Her hands fluttered as they rested on her hips wanting to ease the need twisting through her core. Eve licked her lips, biting down to fight the urge to pleasure herself at the sight of Xander jerking off.

"Fuck. Eve," Xander groaned deeply. Eve gasped as Xander moaned her name; she could not look away. Xander's hands sped up, and his head tipped back as he orgasmed, his cum spraying all over the glass of the shower. He moaned her name one more time before slumping under the warm water.

Eve scurried back to her room, her heart rioting in her chest, hoping that Xander remained clueless about what she had just witnessed and what he had done to her. Eve buried herself in her room, her hand slipping below her pants, sliding in her panties, and over her warm pulsing clit. Her fingers deftly worked herself to climax at the memory of Xander coming in the shower. Eve slipped into an orgasm-induced sleep, even though she had just slept the day away. She didn't wake up once in the night. It took Eve a moment to remember her late-night shenanigans as she woke up. Time seemed to move differently in the Pod. She was stuck in one small apartment with nothing but work or fucking her match to do. She had worked more hours this week and gotten more sleep then back at home this first week

Eve got out of bed, calming her flaming face, to face the piper. Xander was sipping his coffee, his notebook sitting in front of him. He looked all sexy smart as he scribbled away at it.

"Morning." Eve turned to pour herself a coffee.

"Morning." Xander didn't seem any different from any other morning. Eve sipped her coffee, watching him closely. Noting his every more.

"I saw you last night," he revealed quietly. *Oh fuck!* Eve's heart hammered in her ears, and her palms were sweaty, slipping on her coffee cup.

"How long were you there?" Xander asked and didn't look up from his notebook.

"Not long," Eve answered coolly. Xander looked up at her, his eyes unwavering from hers.

"Good. Next time, just knock if you need to use the bathroom; no need to wait so long." Xander smiled at her before returning to his work. Eve's blood pressure started to return to normal, but he didn't realize how much she saw. She slid into the chair next to him, setting her phone next to her coffee cup.

"About yesterday. I am sorry. I guess I just thought we had more than just a match." He closed his book. A deep emotion swam in his eyes, something Eve could not place.

"Oh," she hummed quietly, as her fingers fiddled with her coffee cup. Before she could form a response, her phone started to buzz. Glancing at the phone, the number scrolled across the top. Both of them looked at the phone. She recognized the number of one of her new customers.

"Sorry, I have to take this." Eve got up and escaped to her room before answering the phone.

37

Xander

Xander sat at the table, staring at his coffee as he mulled over the meaning of the phone call. He knew that phone number, but how did she? Xander abandoned his coffee as he pulled out his phone. He could hear the dull sound of Eve talking through her door, but he couldn't make out a word of what she was saying. Xander pulled up the contact for Kenny, ruminating over whether he was going to do this. Eve let out a warm laugh from her room. Xander ground his molars, spurring his fingers into action.

His fingers raced over the screen, a paragraph of rage filling it. Xander was too focused on pouring his feelings into words that adequately housed his feelings; he did not see Eve exit her room.

"What did the poor phone do to you?" she joked as she refilled her coffee mug.

"Huh? Oh. Nothing," Xander laughed. Xander watched her walk back into her room. Xander was transfixed by the swaying of her hips. Xander deleted his rage-filled word vomit from his phone, opting for a simpler question.

Who did you just call?

Kenny

Huh?

You just called someone. Who?

Kenny

Tattoo shop Owner

Xander stared at the words on his phone, letting them sink in. Xander looked up at the closed door that blocked Eve from his view.

What?

Kenny

> *She runs the luxury tattoo parlor that the Spiked Devils like. The one we have been looking for.*

The one we have been looking for, his mind was spinning in his head.

> **Send me the info.**

Kenny

> *Just remember, it took us over six months to get this info. It took me over a month to gain her trust.*

> **She's my match.**

Xander waited, left on read for several long minutes.

Kenny

> *All the info has been emailed to you.*

EVE

Eve sipped her coffee as she drafted an email to her assistant manager, outlining the private booking for next week. A soft knock came from her closed door. Xander was leaning against the door frame as Eve tugged it open, pulling her sweater closer around her.

"How many tattoos do you have?" Xander asked, smiling at her, but his smile did not reach his eyes; there was something darker in his eyes.

"Just the one," Eve said, smiling back.

"Ok," Xander quipped, straightening from the door frame and walking away.

Eve finished up her favorite butternut squash pasta, whipping the bowl clean with a slice of bread.

"Want to fuck in the shower?" Xander asked out of nowhere. Eve sat there chewing her slice of bread, looking at him, thinking.

"That's dangerous," Eve offered up, not a no, but not a yes.

"But it would be so good," he countered.

"I'm not sure." She fidgeted with her sleeve. Looking at her forearm, where she knew a tattoo of a knife sat. A detailed piece that she had designed herself from one of her favorite books.

"Oh, I thought we were only fucking?" Xander said with a little bit of bite to his tone, "so let's fuck." Xander pushed open the bathroom door.

"You can't force me," Eve said, not getting up.

"I'm not. I'm just doing what we are here to do." Xander looked at her, unblinking.

"Right," Eve said, standing up.

"Let's fuck in my room." Eve walked past Xander and into her room.

"Sure." Xander followed her into the room.

"Lights on," Xander said, pulling his shirt off.

"I'd prefer not." Eve stood by her bed fully dressed.

"Why?" he asked. Eve didn't look at Xander, trying to find the words that sounded right. Eve fought her tongue to find the right words.

"Because I don't just have one tattoo. And I'm a private person . . . if we are just fucking like you keep saying. . ." Eve got more worked up the more she talked.

"I don't want to let you in." Eve looked at him, meeting her steely gaze.

"And if we aren't?" Xander whispered.

"I'm not getting my heart broken cause you are lonely —I'm not getting my heart broken when you leave, when we leave the Pod."

Eve panted as she had just emptied her heart onto the floor for him to walk all over. Xander didn't say anything, and all the bravado left Eve, deflating like a popped balloon.

"When I first saw you. . ." Xander started.

"You thought I was pretty or something," Eve interrupted. She frowned at him before starting to walk to the door.

"Yes, but— " Xander tried to say.

"But what?" Eve whipped around to face him, her face warped with a snarl.

"You were wearing a dark blue dress, your hair down, you were reading . . . *A-A Twin's Demise*, I think . . . and I was breathless." Xander followed her to the door.

"That was five years ago," she pointed out.

"I know." Xander just watched her. Something had broken in his eyes, a softness shining through.

"So break my heart because then at least for some time I will be yours. Break my heart because the pain of that is less than the pain of never having you." Xander's voice was soft, but filled with so much conviction. Eve took him in, really took him in.

"I have secrets," Eve whispered.

"So do I, Butterfly," Xander whispered.

"Give me a chance. Give me time, and we can learn from each other." Xander did not move; he looked so raw.

"Ok," Eve agreed. Xander smiled at her, stepping forward.

"Now I am gonna make you come till you beg me to stop." Xander wrapped his arms around Eve, pulling her close.

"The point is for *you* to cum *in me*." Eve laughed as Xander picked her up.

"I will." Xander carried her to his room. Xander gently dropped Eve onto his bed. He crawled on his knees over to her, grabbing her ankles, pulling her legs up, and placing them against his shoulders. Xander quickly tugged Eve's pants off, flinging them to the side. Her panties followed next. Xander settled down, his face only a couple of inches from Eve's pussy. That wicked smirk that Eve had fallen in love with long ago took up Xander's whole face.

Eve's back jumped as Xander's tongue made contact with her skin, one long lick sliding up her cunt and over her clit. A small groan left Xander as he started to lick her over and over again. Eve's fingers gripped Xander's sheets, her feet hooking behind his head, her thighs pressing into his ears.

Eve's back arched, and she let out a low moan as Xander started to suck on her clit.

"Xander," Eve moaned, as he did not let up on her cunt. Her thighs shook a little as they gripped his head. Xander snaked his arm between her legs. His fingers graced over her pussy, before parting her labia, before sliding his finger into her core. Eve gasped as his finger sank deeper into her.

"Eve," Xander whispered into her pussy. He slowly thrust his finger in and out of her, keeping his mouth on her clit. Eve let go of the sheets with one hand, reaching over to grab his hair, pulling his hand closer to her. Xander took his cue and sucked on her clit, picking up speed. Eve was lost in a pool of pleasure, snaking up her body and pooling in her core.

"Xander. Fuck," Eve moaned, letting her weight fall on his shoulders.

Eve's orgasm rolled over her body, her pussy spasming around Xander's finger.

"Such a good girl, Butterfly," Xander cooed, licking her clean. Xander gently guided her legs down, resting beside him, letting her body weight rest fully on the bed.

"How are you doing, Butterfly?" Xander asked, rubbing her thighs.

"Amazing." Eve smiled at him, her face flushed with her orgasm. Eve bit her tongue as Xander rubbed the head of his cock up against her swollen cunt. Eve watched him as he slowly rubbed his cock against her. Xander looked at her as the head of his cock dipped into her. Eve nodded at him. Eve braced herself to take him, and Xander shifted his weight forward. His cock slipped into her wet pussy, taking his full length in one thrust. His right hand slid up her soft side, resting his hand by her shoulder, taking his weight.

"Ready?" Xander asked, looking down at her.

"Yes," Eve whispered, smiling at him.

"You take my cock so well, Butterfly," Xander whispered in her ear right before he thrust into her. Eve's hands whipped up to his back. With each deep thrust, Eve's fingers dug into his back.

"Xander?" Eve asked as he thrust into her.

"Yes?" he asked, stopping.

"Let go. Fuck me with everything you got." Eve dug her fingers into his back to emphasize her point.

"Ok, Butterfly," Xander said, kissing her neck, nipping at her shoulder. Xander took a deep breath, looking into her eyes, and he started to thrust into her. He quickly built speed, sliding into her with more power each time. He kept his weight off her with his right hand, his left gripping her juicy thigh, pulling her into him.

Xander started to pant in her ear, the sound of Eve's moans mixing with the sound of his breathing, twinning with their pleasure.

"Xander." Eve moaned, tipping her head back into his bed. Xander continued to rut into her, his moans joining hers. Xander released her thigh, leaning over, looping a finger around her right wrist, pulling it above her head. She kept her hand where Xander had placed it, even when he released it to get her other wrist. Gently, he held both her hands above her head, one hand just resting on her wrists, as he rutted deep into her.

"Fuck you feel so good, Butterfly," Xander growled into her ear. He leaned over, resting his head on her shoulder as he groaned and panted, his climax close.

"Cum in me," Eve moaned as she tipped over the edge, her orgasm hitting her like a wave. Xander groaned as he gave one last deep thrust before he followed her over the edge as well. Eve felt the gentle pulse as Xander's load filled her up. Xander slumped forward, resting his head in the crook of her shoulder. They stayed there panting, Xander's cock still resting inside of her.

"Butterfly," Xander mumbled, pulling his body off Eve. Eve looked at him, really looked at him, taking in the contours of his face. He placed a gentle kiss on her forehead. She just lay in his bed watching as he cleaned himself up. Wiped down his face with a towel, then rubbed his now softened dick clean. She watched as he pulled on some loose jogging pants sitting low on his hips.

"Here." He handed her one of his shirts. Without getting up, she slipped the soft shirt over her head. The bed dipped as Xander curled up with her in bed. She tumbled into a soft sleep as she cuddled up with Xander.

Eve and Xander spent their days working, and their evenings enjoying dinner together. The late nights were spent between the sheets chasing their pleasures together.

The tablet sitting by the door was blinking bright red. Eve wandered over, nursing her hot mug of coffee. *The required pregnancy test submission is due!* Blinked across the screen over and over again.

"Xander!" she called, tapping at the screen, but the red screen would not clear.

"What's up?" He ambled over.

"Oh," fell out of his mouth as he read the screen.

She dug the specialized pregnancy tests from under the bathroom sink. She chugged back her mug of coffee and then followed it up with two glasses of water. The minutes dragged by as she waited till she needed to pee. After forty-five minutes, she was able to take the test. Xander waited outside the bathroom as she took the test. She walked out and handed him the small white plastic box. He walked over to the tablet and waved it under the scanner. The screen brought up the pregnancy test screen, directing him to place the side with the blue line up to the magnet. Xander tapped the box to the tablet, letting it stick there. Eve hugged Xander from behind, both of them waiting to see the results.

Eve's mind spun as to what would happen if it came back positive. The tablet dinged, and the test dropped to the floor.

"Negative," Xander said, hugging Eve back. Eve looked at the blue text across the screen, the tablet thanking them for the submission of the test. Xander tapped back out of the test application, and the tablet returned to normal.

Life returned to the easy normal they had just started to build. Eve and Xander baked some delicious chocolate chip cookies, but they did not last the day. That night, Eve and Xander braved having sex in the shower. On Sunday, they ventured out of their apartment and checked out the pool, laughing at the sign reminding people not to have sex in the pool. That night, they had a repeat of the sex over the kitchen counter. After a long day of work on Monday, they checked out the library, coming home with an armful of books to read. After spending the rest of the evening reading, they fucked on the couch surrounded by their books. They took Tuesday off work to continue reading, checking out the gym that evening to work off the cookies they had on the weekend. Eve spent most of the time watching Xander lifting weights out of the corner of her eye. That evening was spent tangled in her bed sheets.

She woke in the early hours of the morning, Xander's arm slung over her waist. Her stomach churned, flipping, and bubbling. Eve blotted up and around the corner, barely making it to the toilet before the contents of her stomach came up. Eve felt Xander's gentle hands pulling all her hair out of the way, holding it, and rubbing her back. Eve rested her head on the cold porcelain, taking deep breaths.

"Test." Xander fumbled around under the sink to find one of the many tests. He handed the test to her, but stayed with her. Eve stood up and sat on the toilet, not caring about modesty.

Xander rubbed her shoulder. Eve once again handed Xander the test, and he paused a moment, taking her in, before leaving to go scan the test. The seconds lasted hours as Eve waited to hear about the results. Eve's head spun as another wave of nausea rolled over her. Xander came back in and kissed her forehead.

"And?" Eve asked, looking up at him.

"Positive."

"Did you submit it?" Eve gripped his hand in a death hold.

"Not yet," he said in a small voice.

"Don't," she yelped. Xander didn't say anything else to her; he just silently pulled her into his arms, guiding her back to bed. Wordlessly, they curled up in bed once more, falling into a night-mare-plagued sleep. Partway through the day,

Xander got up and started to clean the apartment as Eve slept. It wasn't until the sun started to set that she stirred.

"Morning, Butterfly." Xander wrapped his arms around a groggy Eve. Eve stayed silent, taking in the feeling of his body pressed to hers.

"What's wrong?" Xander pulled her hair from her face.

"Our time is over," Eve said, not looking at him as she buried her head in his arms.

"It's only just starting."

"Design me a tattoo." Xander lifted her chin, gazing down at her stunning eyes.

"What?" She frowned at him.

"Design me a tattoo, then we will take another test and submit it." Xander picked up a notebook and pen, handing them both to her.

"Ok."

"And then when we get out of here, you will tattoo me." Xander flipped open the notebook.

"Really?" Eve looked up at him.

"I'm not going anywhere," Xander reassured. She leaned over and placed a fluttering kiss on his lips. She settled down on the couch, flipping the pen between her fingers, thinking, staring blankly at the page. Hours ticked by, and he watched her over the top of his laptop. Now and then, she would sketch a couple of lines, then stare at the page. She felt so uncertain about her future, but this small cross over in their lives made her feel like it was possible.

"Done." She got up and plopped down next to him, passing the notebook over. The page was filled with a stunning black and white line drawing. In the center sat a large butterfly, sitting behind the butterfly was an hourglass, the sand falling through the hourglass and out around the butterfly into an infinity sign. Xander took in the drawing as Eve got up and went to the bathroom. She needed to take a new test as they had waited too long since she took the other one —it would come back inconclusive. Eve walked out of the bathroom moments later, and he had not moved; he didn't even look up at her as she started towards the tablet, scanning the new test.

Eve gently pressed submit, waiting to see what happened. Eve settled down on the couch, crossing her legs.

"What do you think?" she asked, he finally looked up at Eve.

"I love it." Xander smiled at her.

"Where would you like it?" She asked as she ran her fingers over the paper.

"On my forearm." Xander ran his hand over the blank skin on his right forearm.

The tablet beeped at them, back to the flashing red screen; this time, it had different text on it. *An appointment with a doctor has been booked for 4 P.M. today.* Eve exited the screen and pulled up the map to see where the doctor's office was. It was five floors down, and she had over an hour before she needed to leave.

"Snack?" Xander asked her, resting his hands on her hips. She couldn't turn down him feeding her—it was their love language.

"Yes." Eve leaned against him. By the time they had made and eaten their snack of pizza wraps, the hour had nearly lapsed.

"Do you want me to come with you?" Xander asked, looking at the clock.

"Would you?" Eve pulled on her sweater.

"Always." Xander pulled on a sweater himself. They left hand in hand, walking down the stairs to the doctor's office. The waiting room was empty, except for six plastic red chairs along the wall, interrupted by three evenly spaced white doors. Eve and Xander sank into the chairs, looking at each other. Neither broke the silence as they waited for an untold amount of time.

"Eve?" A small black woman peeked her head out of one of the doors.

"Yes." Eve stood up. She glanced back at Xander, who smiled at her as she was led into another room.

"Sit here, my dear." She patted the exam table. Eve settled on top of the paper sheet that rested on the table.

"The doctor will be with you in a moment." She left, leaving Eve alone with nothing but her thoughts. What felt like hours later, but was probably only a couple of minutes, a tall Latina woman came in. She was dressed in a blue pantsuit and a white coat. She was drop dead gorgeous.

"We will be doing two tests and then you can be on your way," she launched into without a greeting.

"A blood test and a scan." She went on putting a cart of supplies closer to her. It only took the doctor a couple of minutes to complete each test.

"You can return to your room; the results will be sent up to you when they are ready." She flashed Eve a warm smile as she left.

Xander wrapped his arms around Eve as they walked back home. Eve checked the tablet as soon as they walked in the door, there was no update. Eve slumped into the couch, rubbing her face.

"Here," Xander said as he handed her a glass of water, before settling down next to her. They sat there together for what felt like over an hour not saying anything to each other. Eve leaned over and flicked his forearm.

"Ouch," Xander hissed, flinching, looking at her.

"Tattoos gonna hurt there," she replied, smiling at him. The musical ding of the tablet chimed, interrupting Eve's giggles. They stopped and looked at each other, the room painfully silent. Eve stood up, walking over to the tablet. *Check the mail slot.* It was the only message on the screen. Xander stepped out of the room, pulling a package of papers with him. Eve ripped open the seal, tugging out the papers. The first page listed the test results. *Positive.*

The next pages were pamphlets, and the last were some paperwork. *The Pen.* Written across the top of the page. The Pen was where the expecting mothers were housed until the birth of their child. The child would then be handed to the state, which would raise them. There was no paperwork for Eve; it was all for Xander, but the pamphlets were all for Eve. Eve read through them as Xander frowned at the paperwork; it wasn't anything Eve didn't already know.

Eve watched Xander as he signed the bottom of the page.

"What did you choose?" Eve asked, looking at him.

"The only choice," he answered, smiling.

"I'm staying with you." They both stare down at the paperwork, waiting for the other to break the silence. The paperwork Xander had filled out.

"Before I submit these, there is one thing you should know," Xander said, not looking up.

"Yes?" Eve looked at him, watching every little movement on his face.

"The business I run," he started.

"The gym?" Eve frowned.

"Yes. It's a front," Xander admitted and still didn't look at her, his thumb worrying the edge of the paper.

"I know," Eve said, still watching him.

"You do?" he asked, finally looking up at her. She did, she had known for several months ever since one of his co-workers had come digging around her shop.

"You run the Skinned Demons fight club." He just looked at her blankly, his jaw slack. He had been stunned into stupidity, his brain process her words.

"I do. How did you know?" he asked, looking at her concerned.

"I walk in similar circles," Eve explained. A few beats passed before Eve started to explain.

After half an hour of Eve hashing out her past, which brought her to where she was today. She fidgeted, waiting, hoping that her past wasn't too much. Eve blinked as Xander leaned over, gently pressing his lips to hers. Seconds passed as he kept kissing her softly, building heat as their lips got feverish with need.

"Ready for your next ink?" Eve asked against this lip.

"Very." Xander smiled at her. "Let's go, Butterfly."